A SEASON OF JOY

For my parents, who have always made Christmas the most special time of year.

—D.A.

For my parents, Robert and Mary San Souci, and my mother-in-law, Patricia Colosimo.

—D.S.S.

A SEASON OF JOY

Favorite Stories and Poems for Christmas

COMPILED AND EDITED BY DIANE ARICO

ILLUSTRATED BY DANIEL SAN SOUCI

 Doubleday NEW YORK LONDON TORONTO SYDNEY AUCKLAND

Published by Doubleday, a division of
Bantam Doubleday Dell Publishing Group, Inc.,
666 Fifth Avenue, New York, New York 10103

Doubleday and the portrayal of an anchor with a dolphin
are trademarks of Doubleday, a division of
Bantam Doubleday Dell Publishing Group, Inc.

Acknowledgments

"The Barn" by Elizabeth Coatsworth reprinted by permission of Coward-McCann from *Compass Rose* by Elizabeth Coatsworth, copyright © 1929 by Coward, McCann, Inc., copyright renewed © 1957 by Elizabeth Coatsworth.

"The Christmas Spider" from *Up the Hill* by Marguerite de Angeli. Copyright © 1942 by Marguerite de Angeli. Reprinted by permission of Doubleday & Company, Inc.

"The Dwarf and the Cobbler's Sons" from *Tales That Nimko Told* by Mary Brecht Pulver. Copyright © 1925 by The Century Co., renewed 1953 by Gordon W. Pulver. A Hawthorn Book. Reprinted by permission of E. P. Dutton, a division of New American Library.

"The Little Blind Shepherd": Adaptation from *Follow the Star* copyright © 1980 by Mala Powers. Adapted with permission from "The Little Blind Shepherd" copyright © 1959 by George Sharp; first published in *It's Time for Christmas* edited by Elizabeth Hough Sechrist and Janette Woolsey.

"The Little Drummer Boy": Copyright © 1958 (Renewed) by Mills Music, Inc., and International Korwin Corp., and WB Music Corp. Used with permission. All Rights Reserved.

While every effort has been made to obtain permission, there may still be cases in which we have failed to trace a copyright holder, and we would like to apologize for any apparent negligence.

Text copyright © 1987 by Doubleday & Company, Inc.
Illustrations copyright © 1987 by Daniel San Souci

Library of Congress Cataloging-in-Publication Data

A season of joy.

Summary: An illustrated collection of short stories,
poems, and excerpts from longer works on a Christmas
theme.
1. Christmas—Literary collections. [1. Christmas—
Literary collections] I. San Souci, Daniel, ill.
II. Arico, Diane.
PZ5.S4368 1987   808.8′033   86-29059
ISBN: 0-385-23901-7
ISBN: 0-385-23902-5 (lib. bdg.)

Printed in the United States of America
4   6   8   9   7   5   3
HL

CONTENTS

The Barn

by ELIZABETH COATSWORTH

"I am tired of this barn!" said the colt.
  "And every day it snows.
Outside there's no grass any more
  And icicles grow on my nose.
I am tired of hearing the cows
  Breathing and talking together.
I am sick of these clucking hens.
  I *hate* stables and winter weather!"

"Hush, little colt," said the mare,
  "And a story I will tell
Of a barn like this one of ours
  And the wonders that there befell.
It was weather much like this,
  And the beasts stood as we stand now
In the warm good dark of the barn—
  A horse and an ass and a cow."

6

"And sheep?" asked the colt. "Yes, sheep
   And a pig and a goat and a hen—
All of the beasts of the barnyard,
   The usual servants of men.
And into their midst came a lady,
   And she was as cold as death,
But the animals leaned above her
   And made her warm with their breath.

"There was her baby born
   And laid to sleep in the hay
While music flooded the rafters
   And the barn was as light as day.
And angels and kings and shepherds
   Came to worship the Babe from afar,
But we looked at Him first of all creatures
   By the bright strange light of a star!"

The Dwarf
and the Cobbler's Sons
by MARY BRECHT PULVER

A long time ago there lived in Friesland a poor cobbler and his three little boys, Franz, Friedrich, and Fritz.

He was a very poor cobbler indeed. He had scarcely any shoes whatever to mend, and times were very hard and the winter bitter cold, with heavy snow upon the ground.

In the cobbler's house were only the poorest sort of things, not in the least like the things you are used to. There was no bed like yours, with plenty of warm covering to snuggle into on cold nights.

The three boys slept together on a thin cold bed of straw and had for cover only a single blanket as full of holes as a slice of Swiss cheese. And their clothes were hardly any better, so, as you may imagine, they did a great deal of shivering.

As for food, the best the poor cobbler could manage that winter were lumps of boiled cornmeal, a delicacy I am sure you would never care for.

Now, as Christmas approached, the cobbler's three sons felt sad, for they feared the good Kris Kringle might miss them, which in those days sometimes happened.

But on Christmas Eve the cobbler got tidings of a bit of work to be done twenty miles away, where a fine lady had lost a button from her little silver dancing shoes, so he said to his boys:

"My lads, I will leave you for tonight. Tomorrow is the Christ Child's birthday and perhaps if I hasten to this lady's house and repair her shoe, I may yet have a *farden* or two to buy a bit of good food with. It is a long journey and I will not return until morning, but lie you snug and close as you can under the blanket. And let no one enter in my absence, for the wolf prowls ever at the poor man's door, and the cold winds may rush in and make you even colder."

And the little lads promised.

So the cobbler gave to each a lump of cornmeal, the last the poor man had, and wrapping himself in his thin cloak—for all the world like another slice of Swiss cheese—was gone.

The three boys huddled together in bed very quietly, nibbling their meal. They had little Fritz in the middle, and they tried hard to pretend they were warm and comfortable. But it was very cold and they could hear the wind blow, "Whoo-oo-oo! Whoo-oo!" and through their little window they could see the bright stars shining in the cold blue sky.

Suddenly there came a brisk knock—Tat-tat! Tat-tat!—right on the outside of their door.

The boys were startled.

"It must be the wolf that our father said waited outside," whispered Franz, but Friedrich called loudly:

"Who is there?"

"Ah, me! Ah, me!" cried a pitiful voice. "I am so cold! So c-oo-oold! And I am so hungry! Pray let me come in!"

"It is the wind," said little Franz.

"No, no," said Friedrich. "It must be someone in distress. Who are you?" he called.

"Ah, me! Ah, me!" shivered the voice. "So co-o-old, so tired, so hungry! Pray let me in!"

"It is the wolf, perhaps, trying to fool us," said Franz.

"Oh no," said Friedrich. "Look out of the window, Franz, quick, and see."

Franz looked. In the corner of the window they could see the top of a peaked hat—such a hat as poor old men used to wear many, many years ago in Germany.

"It cannot be the wolf," cried Franz. "A wolf never wears a hat." And I am sure you will agree with him.

"It is someone who needs our aid," said Friedrich. "I am sure our father never meant us to deny shelter to the needy." And with that he rose and opened the door.

Into the room sprang one of the dwarf people, a tiny old man clad in scarlet, with twinkling eyes, apple cheeks, and a gray beard that reached nearly to his toes.

"Hola!" he said. "At last you hear me and let me in. Why did you not open before?"

"Our father forbade us to open the door, for fear of the wolf. I am sorry," faltered Friedrich.

The dwarf only twinkled his eyes angrily.

"Ha!" he cried. "A warm bed and three great loafers in it! Make way, I pray, for I am cold and tired."

And, shoving aside Franz and Fritz with his elbows, he sprang into the warmest part of the bed and rolled the blanket tightly about him.

Little Fritz began to cry, but Friedrich hushed him, saying:

"Patience, brother. I will wrap my coat about you. The old man is both tired and cold, and our father would wish us to share our bed."

The dwarf then perceived the cornmeal in the children's hands and snatched greedily at it, saying:

"Come, selfish ones, will you lie here and fill yourselves with good food before my very eyes! Have I not said that I am hungry?"

He made as if to take Fritz's cornmeal, so that the little boy wept again, whereupon Friedrich offered his.

"He is but a baby, the little one, and knows no better," he apologized. "Pray have mine. Our father would not have us let a guest go hungry."

So the dwarf ate both Franz's and Friedrich's cornmeal, then rolled over to his side, complaining bitterly that they crowded him, that he must have more room.

Suddenly he sat erect.

"There is not room for so many," he said sharply. "One of you will have to get out. You, Friedrich, are the eldest. You shall go first. The others may take turns. Go you to yonder corner and stand upon your head."

Now Friedrich thought this a strange request indeed. It was bad enough to leave his bed, without turning upside down. But he was a polite little fellow, and just a bit afraid, also, of this sharp-tongued little man, so he obeyed. Down on his hands he went and up . . . up . . . up went his heels!

Instantly there came a funny sound. Pop-pop! pop-pop! thump, thump, thump! tap! tap! went something, and there, down on the bare wooden floor, dropping from his pockets, came a perfect torrent of nuts and apples and oranges. Oh, every kind of nut you have ever heard of— hickory nuts, walnuts, chestnuts, butternuts, peanuts, right down to the end of the list—great handfuls of them, and apples by the dozen, fat and rosy. And oranges, great bounding golden fellows. You may be sure there was a shouting then and a leaping to capture these fine treasures.

"Hello!" cried the dwarf. "So that is what you have hidden from me, my fine lad! Let us see what the rest of you have. Franz, you next."

Down on his hands went Franz and up . . . up . . . went his heels.

Sure enough! His pockets, too, seemed to be filled, for, with a rat-tat-tat, down on the floor came a stream of bright candies. Oh, my! I cannot tell all the kinds! Think of every kind you like, of every kind you know. There were chocolates bursting with cream, mints and marshmallows, great lumps of taffy and fudge, limedrops and gumdrops, and—but what is the use! There was enough for a whole confectioner's shop.

Now, you may be sure, the brothers laughed and shouted louder than ever as they gathered up the goodies.

"Small Fritz next," shouted the dwarf, who seemed angry with Franz for hiding such goodies.

They had to help Fritz because he was so small. Down on his hands he went and up they turned his little heels.

You'll hardly believe what happened then. Dear me! If you and I could have such luck! (But think how pleased the good cobbler was when he returned.) For out of Fritz's pockets—clip-clop! clip-clop!—

sharp on the floor there fell . . . money. Beautiful gold thalers—enough for firewood and blankets, and new shoes and coats and a fine roast Christmas goose.

Suddenly Friedrich remembered his manners, for he knew now that the dwarf had come in with kind intentions, that he had tested their charity and found it true. For had they not shared their best and the things they had themselves needed?

"Oh, sir, we thank you," he began, then stopped, as well he might.

For the dwarf was gone.

Not a sign of the little gray-bearded man in his scarlet clothes could they find. Nor did they ever see him again.

But a voice cried through the window from outside, "A happy Christmas to the cobbler and his three sons." And that was all. Except, of course, all the beautiful things to eat and piles of golden thalers which made their poor little room so bright.

The Little Blue Dishes

AUTHOR UNKNOWN

Once upon a time there was a poor woodcutter who lived with his wife and three children in a little cabin in the forest. There was a big boy named John and a little boy named Peter, and a dear little girl named Gretchen, just five years old.

Christmas was coming, and the children went to the village toy shop to look at all the toys. There were tops and balls and blocks. There were woolly bears and other stuffed animals, and also animals made of wood. There were all kinds of dolls, and there was furniture for dollhouses— and many other things.

"Gretchen," said Peter, "what do you like best?"

"Oh, that little box of blue dishes!" said Gretchen. "That is the best of all." She could not take her eyes off the cunning teapot, the sugar bowl and cream pitcher, and the two little cups and saucers.

On Christmas Eve the children hung up their stockings, although their mother had told them they must not expect much this year.

After supper John ran out to play with the big boys. Gretchen and Peter sat by the fire talking about the toys they had seen.

"I wish I had those little blue dishes," said Gretchen. But soon she became sleepy and went off to bed.

Peter ran to look at his bank. He found only one penny, but he took it and ran to the toy shop. "What can I buy for a penny?" he asked the toy man.

"You can buy a little candy heart with a picture on it," said the man.

"But I want that set of blue dishes," said Peter.

"Oh, those cost ten cents," said the man.

"Well, then I'll take the candy heart," said Peter. He took it home and put it in the toe of Gretchen's stocking and then he went to bed.

Pretty soon, John came home. He was cold and hungry. While he was warming himself by the fire, he noticed the lump in Gretchen's stocking. He put in his hand and drew out the candy heart. "Oh," said John, "how good this smells!" And before he thought about what he was doing, he ate the candy heart. "Oh dear," he thought, "that was for Gretchen for Christmas. I must run and buy something else for her."

He ran to get his bank and he found he had ten pennies. Quickly he ran to the toy shop. The man was just ready to close up. "What have you for ten pennies?" he asked the storekeeper.

"Well, I'm almost sold out," said the toy man, "but here is a little set of blue dishes."

"I will take them," said John, and he ran home and put them in Gretchen's stocking. Then he went to bed.

Early Christmas morning the children jumped out of bed and came running to look at their stockings.

"Oh," cried Gretchen, "look at my stocking!" She had found the blue dishes and she was dancing for joy. But Peter could never understand how his candy heart changed into a box of blue dishes!

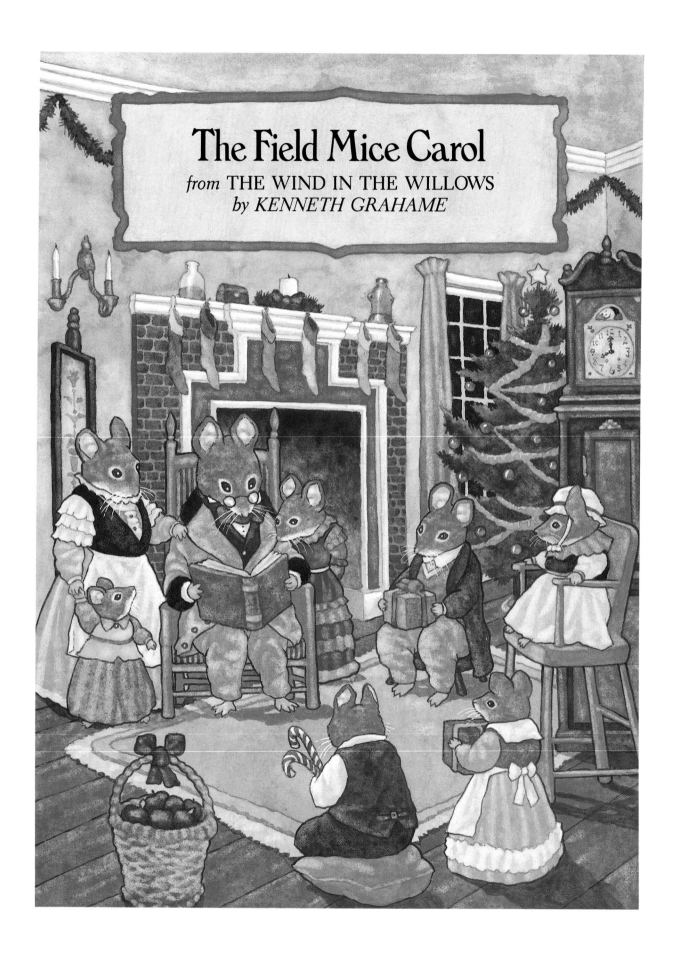

The Field Mice Carol

from THE WIND IN THE WILLOWS
by KENNETH GRAHAME

Villagers all, this frosty tide,
Let your doors swing open wide,
Though wind may follow, and snow beside,
Yet draw us in by your fire to bide;
　　Joy shall be yours in the morning!

Here we stand in the cold and the sleet,
Blowing fingers and stamping feet,
Come from far away you to greet—
You by the fire and we in the street—
　　Bidding you joy in the morning!

For ere one half of the night was gone,
Sudden a star has led us on,
Raining bliss and benison—
Bliss tomorrow and more anon,
　　Joy for every morning!

Goodman Joseph toiled through snow—
Saw the star o'er a stable low;
Mary she might not further go—
Welcome thatch and litter below!
　　Joy was hers in the morning!

And then they heard the angels tell
"Who were the first to cry Nowell?
Animals all, as it befell,
In the stable where they did dwell!
　　Joy shall be theirs in the morning!"

The Little Blind Shepherd

Adaptation by MALA POWERS

Long ago, near the town of Bethlehem, there lived a young blind boy named Thaddy. He was a kind and happy child and loved to go into the hills with his father to tend their sheep. He was also a wonderfully capable boy who, even though blind, planted his own garden and sold his fresh-picked vegetables at the marketplace in Bethlehem.

One bitter winter afternoon, as he was returning home from the marketplace with his donkey, Petra, Thaddy heard the voices of a man and a woman on the road ahead. As he passed them, the woman stumbled and fell.

"Are you hurt, Mary?" Thaddy heard the man ask anxiously.

"No, Joseph, but I fear I cannot walk even a little farther. I ache so with the cold."

"Can I help you?" Thaddy called out. "My home is near here."

"You are very kind," replied the lady, "but my husband and I must reach Bethlehem before dark."

It was so cold and the lady sounded so weary that Thaddy's heart went out to her. "Please take my donkey. You can return him to me in a few days."

The lady smiled and said gently, "Why, bless you, little one. But what would your parents say?"

"Oh, Petra is mine!" said Thaddy. "I bought him with my own money. My parents will understand when I tell them I lent Petra to a sweet-sounding lady who needed him. Don't worry. I can find my way very well without him."

The lady drew in a quick breath. "Oh, Joseph," she exclaimed, "the boy is blind. Is it right that we should accept his kindness?"

The man's voice came quietly. "Perhaps it is a sign, Mary." And turning to Thaddy, he said, "God bless you for your kindness, my son."

And Thaddy's heart was strangely glad as the lady rode off to Bethlehem on little Petra.

That night Thaddy went with his father to the hills to watch over their sheep. As they stood with the other shepherds, a great stillness came upon them. Suddenly the cold night air was filled with a strange sound, and the shepherds called out in fear. Then Thaddy heard the voice of an angel saying, "Fear not, for behold, I bring you tidings of great joy, which shall be to all people. For unto you is born, this day, in the city of David, a Savior, which is Christ the Lord. You shall find the babe wrapped in swaddling clothes, lying in a manger."

And suddenly, there was with the angel a multitude of the heavenly host saying, "Glory to God in the highest, and on earth peace, good will toward men." Then the vision of the angels dissolved into a bright and glittering star which the shepherds followed to a stable in Bethlehem.

As they entered the stable and crowded lovingly round the sleeping child, Mary's glowing eyes fell upon Thaddy.

"Why, you are the blind boy who gave us your donkey so that my journey might be easier. Reach out your arms. I will let you hold my son."

And as Thaddy held the precious bundle to his heart, his world grew bright and warm. The light became form, the form took shape, and the shape was the Christ Child lying peacefully in his arms.

For a long moment, Thaddy looked at the Christ Child in wonder, then whispered, "My lady, I can see him! With my eyes, I can see him! I do not understand, but I can see!"

When at last the shepherds took their leave, Thaddy turned to Joseph. "You will need my little donkey, Petra," he said. "Please keep him. I would like him to be *my* gift."

The Jar of Rosemary

by MAUD LINDSAY

There was once a young prince whose mother, the queen, was sick. All summer she lay in bed, and everything was kept quiet in the palace; but when the autumn came she grew better. Every day brought color to her cheeks and strength to her limbs, and by and by the young prince was allowed to go into her room and stand beside her bed to talk to her.

He was very glad of this, for he wanted to ask her what she would like for a Christmas present; and as soon as he had kissed her and laid his cheek against hers, he whispered his question in her ear.

"What should I like for a Christmas present?" said the queen. "A smile and a kiss and a hug around the neck; these are the dearest gifts I know."

But the prince was not satisfied with this answer. "Smiles and kisses and hugs you can have every day," he said, "but think, Mother, think, if you could choose the thing you wanted most in all the world, what would you take?"

"If I might take my choice of all the world I believe a little jar of rosemary like that which bloomed in my mother's window when I was a little girl would please me better than anything else."

The prince was delighted to hear this, and as soon as he had gone out of the queen's room he sent a servant to his father's greenhouses to inquire for a rosemary plant.

But the servant came back with disappointing news. There were carnation pinks in the king's greenhouses and roses with golden hearts, and lovely lilies; but there was no rosemary. Rosemary was a common herb and grew mostly in country gardens, so the king's gardeners said.

"Then go into the country for it," said the young prince. "No matter where it grows, my mother must have it for a Christmas present."

So messengers went into the country here, there, and everywhere to seek the plant, but each one came back with the same story to tell; there was rosemary, enough and to spare, in the spring, but the frost had been in the country and there was not a green sprig left to bring to the young prince for his mother's Christmas present.

Two days before Christmas, however, news was brought that rosemary had been found, a lovely green plant growing in a jar, right in the very city where the prince himself lived.

"But where is it?" said he. "Why have you not brought it with you? Go and get it at once."

"Well, as for that," said the servant who had found the plant, "there is a little difficulty. The old woman to whom the rosemary belongs did not want to sell it even though I offered her a handful of silver for it."

"Then give her a purse of gold," said the prince.

So a purse filled so full of gold that it could not hold another piece was taken to the old woman, but presently it was brought back. She would not sell her rosemary; no, not even for a purse of gold.

"Perhaps if Your Highness would go yourself and ask her, she might change her mind," said the prince's nurse. So the royal carriage drawn by six white horses was brought, and the young prince and his servants rode away to the old woman's house, and when they got there the first thing they spied was the little green plant in a jar standing in the old woman's window.

The old woman herself came to the door, and she was glad to see the prince. She invited him in, and bade him warm his hands by the fire, and gave him a cookie from her cupboard to eat.

She had a young grandson no older than the prince, but he was sick and could not run about and play like other children. He lay in a little white bed in the old woman's room, and the prince, after he had eaten the cookie, spoke to him, and took out his favorite plaything, which he always carried in his pocket, and showed it to him.

The prince's favorite plaything was a ball which was like no other ball that had ever been made. It was woven of magic stuff as bright as the sunlight, as sparkling as the starlight, and as golden as the moon at harvest time. And when the prince threw it into the air or bounced it on the floor or turned it in his hands it rang like a chime of silver bells.

The sick child laughed to hear it and held out his hands for it, and the prince let him hold it, which pleased the grandmother as much as the child.

But pleased though she was, she would not sell the rosemary. She had brought it from the home where she had lived when her grandson's father was a boy, she said, and she hoped to keep it till she died. So the prince and his servants had to go home without it.

No sooner had they gone than the sick child began to talk of the wonderful ball.

"If I had such a ball to hold in my hand," he said, "I should be contented all the day."

"You may as well wish for the moon in the sky," said his grandmother; but she thought of what he said, and in the evening when he was asleep she put her shawl around her, and taking the jar of rosemary with her, she hastened to the king's palace.

When she got there the servants asked her errand, but she would answer nothing till they had taken her to the young prince.

"Silver and gold would not buy the rosemary," she said when she saw him, "but if you will give me your golden ball for my grandchild, you may have the plant."

"But my ball is the most wonderful ball that was ever made!" cried the prince, "and it is my favorite plaything. I would not give it away for anything."

And so the old woman had to go home with her jar of rosemary under her shawl.

The next day was the day before Christmas, and there was a great stir and bustle in the palace. The queen's physician had said that she might sit up to see the Christmas tree that night, and have her presents with the rest of the family; and everyone was running to and fro to get things ready for her.

The queen had so many presents, and very fine they were too, that the Christmas tree could not hold them all, so they were put on a table before the throne and wreathed around with holly and with pine. The young prince went in with his nurse to see them, and to put his gift, which was a jewel, among them.

"She wanted a jar of rosemary," he said as he looked at the glittering heap.

"She will never think of it again when she sees these things. You may be sure of that," said the nurse.

But the prince was not sure. He thought of it himself many times that day, and once, when he was playing with his ball, he said to the nurse:

"If I had a rosemary plant, I'd be willing to sell it for a purse full of gold. Wouldn't you?"

"Indeed yes," said the nurse, "and so would anyone else in his right senses. You may be sure of that."

The boy was not satisfied, though, and presently when he had put his ball up and stood at the window watching the snow which had come to whiten the earth for Christ's birthday, he said to the nurse:

"I wish it were spring. It is easy to get rosemary then, is it not?"

"Your Highness is like the king's parrot that knows but one word with your rosemary, rosemary, rosemary," said the nurse, who was a little out

of patience by that time. "Her Majesty the queen only asked for it to please you. You may be sure of that."

But the young prince was not sure; and when the nurse had gone to her supper and he was left by chance for a moment alone, he put on his coat of fur, and, taking the ball with him, he slipped away from the palace and hastened toward the old woman's house.

He had never been out at night by himself before, and he might have felt a little afraid had it not been for the friendly stars that twinkled in the sky above him.

"We will show you the way," they seemed to say; and he trudged on bravely in their light, till, by and by, he came to the house and knocked at the door.

Now the sick child had been talking of the wonderful ball all evening. "Did you see how it shone, Grandmother? And did you hear how the little bells rang?" he said; and it was just then that the prince knocked at the door.

The old woman made haste to answer the knock, and when she saw the prince she was too astonished to speak.

"Here is the ball," he cried, putting it into her hands. "Please give me the rosemary for my mother."

And so it happened that when the queen sat down before her great table of gifts the first thing she spied was a jar of sweet rosemary like that which had bloomed in her mother's window when she was a little girl.

"I should rather have it than all the other gifts in the world," she said; and she took the young prince in her arms and kissed him.

The Night Before Christmas

by CLEMENT CLARKE MOORE

'Twas the night before Christmas, when all through the house
Not a creature was stirring, not even a mouse;
The stockings were hung by the chimney with care,
In hopes that St. Nicholas soon would be there;
The children were nestled all snug in their beds,
While visions of sugar-plums danced in their heads;
And mamma in her 'kerchief and I in my cap,
Had just settled our brains for a long winter's nap,
When out on the lawn there arose such a clatter,
I sprang from the bed to see what was the matter.
Away to the window I flew like a flash,
Tore open the shutters, and threw up the sash.
The moon, on the breast of the new-fallen snow,
Gave a lustre of mid-day to objects below;
When what to my wondering eyes should appear,
But a miniature sleigh and eight tiny reindeer,
With a little old driver, so lively and quick,
I knew in a moment it must be St. Nick.
More rapid than eagles his coursers they came,
And he whistled, and shouted, and called them by name;
"Now, Dasher! now, Dancer! now, Prancer and Vixen!
On, Comet! on, Cupid! on, Donner and Blitzen!

To the top of the porch! to the top of the wall!
Now, dash away, dash away, dash away all!"
As dry leaves that before the wild hurricane fly,
When they meet with an obstacle, mount to the sky,
So up to the house-top the coursers they flew,
With the sleigh full of toys and St. Nicholas too.
And then, in a twinkling, I heard on the roof
The prancing and pawing of each little hoof.
As I drew in my head, and was turning around,
Down the chimney St. Nicholas came with a bound.
He was dressed all in fur, from his head to his foot,
And his clothes were all covered with ashes and soot;
A bundle of toys he had flung on his back,
And he looked like a peddler just opening his pack.
His eyes—how they twinkled! his dimples how merry!
His cheeks were like roses, his nose like a cherry;
His droll little mouth was drawn up like a bow,
And the beard on his chin was as white as the snow;
The stump of a pipe he held tight in his teeth,
And the smoke, it encircled his head like a wreath:
He had a broad face, and a little round belly
That shook, when he laughed, like a bowlful of jelly.
He was chubby and plump, a right jolly old elf,
And I laughed when I saw him, in spite of myself;
A wink of his eye and a twist of his head
Soon gave me to know I had nothing to dread;
He spoke not a word, but went straight to his work,
And filled all the stockings; then turned with a jerk,
And laying his finger aside of his nose,
And giving a nod, up the chimney he rose;
He sprang to his sleigh, to his team gave a whistle,
And away they all flew like the down of a thistle.
But I heard him exclaim, ere he drove out of sight,
"Happy Christmas to all, and to all a good-night."

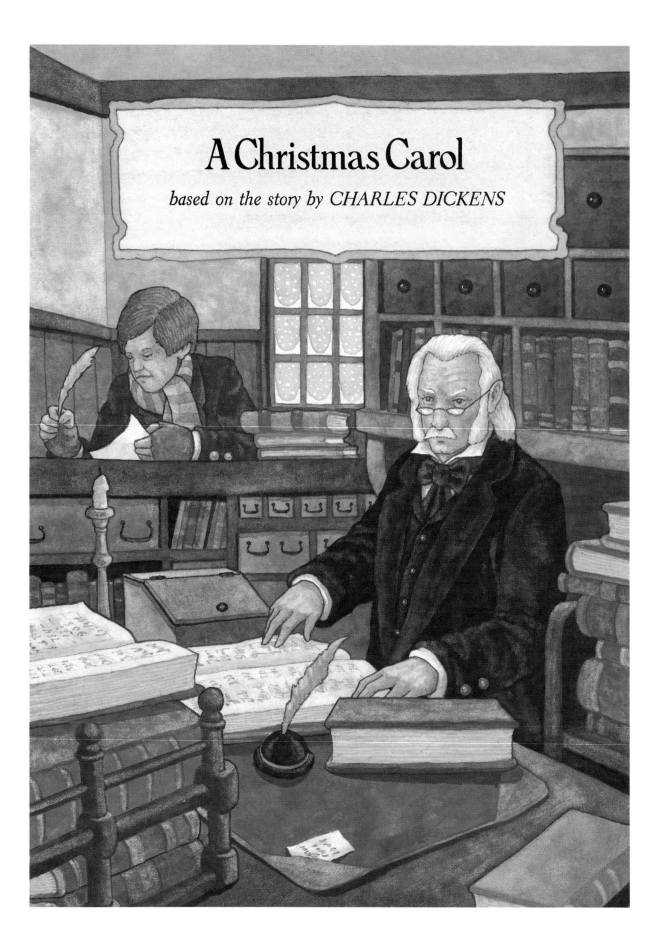

A Christmas Carol

based on the story by CHARLES DICKENS

Once there was a wretched, greedy old sinner named Ebenezer Scrooge. His only joy in life was making money and that he did through his firm of Scrooge & Marley. But his partner, Jacob Marley, had been dead for seven years now. Scrooge lived alone and disliked everyone. He thought of most people as fools, especially at Christmas time when men, women, and children opened their hearts to give gifts and make merry.

"Bah, humbug!" Scrooge would exclaim whenever anyone tried to speak to him about Christmas spirit. He swore never to spend his beloved money on such foolishness as gifts. But then—Scrooge had no one to buy gifts for.

He had a clerk in his office named Bob Cratchit, and he only paid the poor fellow a few shillings a week to feed his wife and family. Whenever Bob took time from his work to warm his hands over the tiny bit of coal that lay in the coal box, Scrooge would chide him relentlessly.

"Back to your work, Bob Cratchit!" Scrooge would snap. "I don't intend to pay you a day's wages for no work."

The young clerk would try to explain that he could barely hold a pencil, his hands were so numb, but Scrooge would cast him a piercing look and scare the poor man half to death.

It was Christmas Eve and into the office of Scrooge & Marley popped Scrooge's nephew, Fred.

"A Merry Christmas, Uncle," Fred offered cheerfully. "God bless you."

"Bah, humbug!" Scrooge snapped.

"Christmas a humbug, Uncle? You don't mean that, I'm sure."

"I DO!" Scrooge yelled. "Merry Christmas, indeed. What right have you to be merry? You're certainly poor enough."

"Oh, come now, Uncle. What right have you to be dismal? You're rich enough."

"Bah, humbug!" Scrooge answered again with the usual response.

"Uncle," Fred continued, "Christmas is the only time of year I know of when men and women open their hearts freely. And though it has never made me rich, I know it *has* done me good, and *will* do me good; and I say, God bless it!"

"Good for you lad," Cratchit called from his desk.

Scrooge turned on his clerk instantly. "Another word from you, Cratchit, and you can be sure that you'll lose your position!"

"Oh, don't be so cross, Uncle," defended Fred.

"WHAT ELSE CAN I BE when I live in such a world of fools as this!" Scrooge yelled. "What's Christmas time to you except a time to pay bills without money! If I could have my way, every idiot who goes about with a Merry Christmas on his lips would be boiled in his own pudding and buried with a stick of holly through his heart."

"Oh, Uncle . . ." Fred said, horrified at his uncle's tirade.

"Keep Christmas in your own way, and let me keep it in mine," said Scrooge.

"But you don't keep it," protested Fred.

"Well, let me leave it alone, then!"

Fred was determined. "Come," he offered his uncle, "dine with us tomorrow."

"Good afternoon," Scrooge said, ignoring his nephew's invitation and pointing to the door to dismiss him.

"Oh, I'm sorry with all my heart to find you so disagreeable," said Fred, "but a Merry Christmas, anyway, Uncle Scrooge."

"Good afternoon," Scrooge repeated, still pointing the way out.

"And a happy New Year!" said Fred.

"GOOD AFTERNOON!" Scrooge yelled.

After his nephew had left, Scrooge eyed his clerk warily. He knew Cratchit was about to ask for Christmas Day off to spend with his family. When the young man approached Scrooge's desk, the old miser had an answer ready.

"Christmas Day is nothing but a poor excuse to pick a man's pocket every December twenty-fifth," he said. "And you, a poor clerk with barely enough money to feed your family talking about a Merry Christmas. Bah, humbug!"

"But, sir," said Bob, "it's Christmas only once a year."

"Yes, I know," said Scrooge, scratching his chin in thought. "Well, I suppose you must have the day off. But be here all the earlier the next morning."

"Oh, indeed I will, sir," Bob answered cheerfully. "Thank you, sir." And with that, Cratchit buttoned his thin tattered overcoat and walked out into the blustery night.

Shortly after, Scrooge left his dreary office and headed home. When he arrived at his front door, however, a most mysterious thing happened. Before Scrooge's very eyes, the door knocker transformed into the face of his dead partner, Jacob Marley. Scrooge shuddered and then looked again at the knocker. To his relief, it had transformed back.

"Bah, humbug!" Scrooge muttered, and up the stairs he went. He put on his dressing gown and sat down before the fire to take his meager dish of gruel. After finishing the simple meal, Scrooge dozed off in his easy chair.

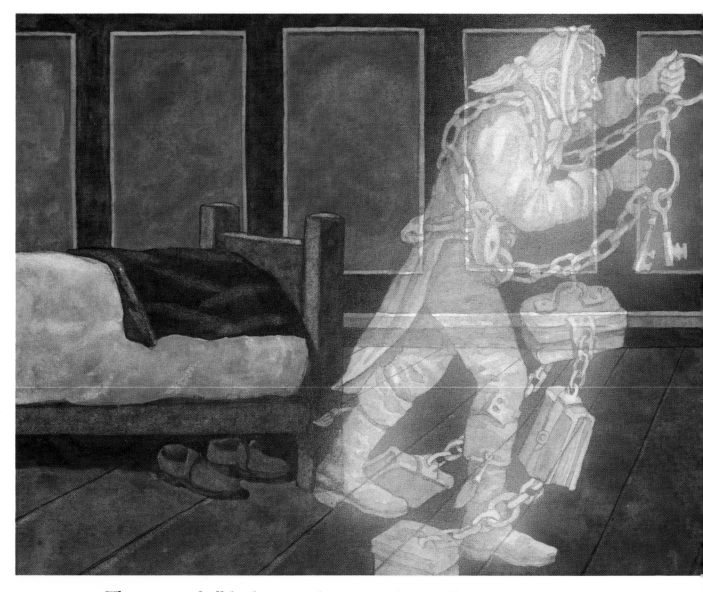

There was a bell high up in the tower of the old house, and it began
to ring, while a noise downstairs made Scrooge wake with a start. The
sound of chains being dragged along the floor came closer and closer.
Suddenly, a ghostly apparition came right through the door and stood
before the frightened old man.

"Aah!" Scrooge gasped. "Who, who are you? What do you want with
me, spirit?"

"I am your partner, Jacob Marley." And with that, the ghost began
rattling the chains that bound him and bellowing in a ghostly voice until
Scrooge could stand it no longer.

"Please, please stop that," he protested. "Jacob, Jacob, settle down.
Speak comfort to me, Jacob."

"I've none to give, Ebenezer Scrooge," the ghost answered. "I've come to warn you of three spirits. Without their visits, you cannot expect to change your evil ways. Expect the first tomorrow when the bell tolls one. The second will come the next night at the same hour. The third on the next night at the last stroke of twelve. You hope to see me no more, but remember what I have said here tonight."

Before Scrooge could answer, the spirit vanished. Scrooge sat there in disbelief, and then denounced the whole thing.

"This business of spirits is rubbish. I won't believe a word of it. Humbug!" Then up the stairs he went and got into bed. He was soon asleep.

The Ghost of Christmas Past

As the chimes of a neighboring church struck twelve, Scrooge awoke. "Hmm, twelve o'clock," he muttered. "Why it can't be! It was past two when I went to bed. Is it possible I've slept through a whole day and into another night? Is it possible that something's happened to the sun and it's twelve noon?"

He got himself up and went to the window. He saw that it was still very dark, so back to bed he went and lay there thinking. As the clock struck one, Scrooge remembered the apparition of Jacob Marley. Marley had warned that the first spirit would come at this very hour.

Suddenly a light flashed within the room and the first of the promised visitors stood before Scrooge.

"Are you the spirit whose coming was foretold to me?" Scrooge asked.

"I am," the spirit answered.

"Who and what are you?" Scrooge asked.

"I am the Ghost of Christmas Past. *Your* past to be exact."

"Well, what business have you got here?" said Scrooge.

"Your welfare is the purpose of my visit," the spirit replied as it walked toward the window and gently stepped onto the ledge. It beckoned Scrooge with one outstretched hand and said, "Rise and walk with me."

Scrooge scurried over to the window, not wanting to cross the ghost, but when he realized what was expected of him he protested.

"But, spirit, I'm mortal and liable to fall."

"Touch my hand," said the spirit, "and you shall be upheld through more than this."

As the words were spoken and Scrooge took the spirit's hand, the two passed through the window and were soon on an open country road with fields on either side.

"Do you know where you are?" the spirit asked.

"Good heavens," said Scrooge. "Of course I do. I was raised in this place. I was a boy here."

"Ah, you recollect the way then?" questioned the spirit.

"I could walk it blindfolded," Scrooge replied.

"You see that schoolhouse over there?" The spirit pointed. "A solitary child neglected by his friends is left there still. Do you know who that boy is?"

"Oh, kind spirit," Scrooge said, his voice quivering with sadness. "It's me. It's my own lost boyhood. My poor forgotten self as I used to be. Ah, me.

"I wish," Scrooge said.

"Wish what?" asked the spirit.

"Ah, nothing, nothing."

"Please tell me," the spirit urged.

"Nothing really," Scrooge said. "It's just that last night a boy came singing a Christmas carol at my front door. I would like to have given him something. That's all."

"Come," said the spirit. "Let us see another Christmas."

This time the spirit took him to the warehouse where Scrooge had been an apprentice. When he saw an old man in a Welsh wig sitting in a high chair, he cried out.

"Why it's ol' Fezziwig! Bless his heart, yes it's ol' Fezziwig alive again. And there's Dick Wilson, dear Dick Wilson, he was a good friend to me."

"Yo ho, my boys, no more work tonight," cried Fezziwig. "Christmas, Ebenezer. Let's have those shutters up."

"Yes, Mr. Fezziwig, it's as good as done."

"Are the floors swept and polished?"

"Yes, sir."

"The lamps trimmed?"

"Oh yes, sir."

"The fuel's on the fire?"

"Yes, sir."

"Hilli-ho! Dick. Chirrup! Ebenezer. The guests will be arriving any minute."

In came a fiddler with a music box. In came Mrs. Fezziwig, smiling brightly. In came all the young men and women employed in the business. They danced and sang, ate and drank, and made merry all the night long. And so the jolly party went on until eleven o'clock, at which point the spirit turned to Scrooge and announced that Fezziwig was a silly man.

"A silly man?" Scrooge protested. "Why he gave everyone much happiness, good spirit. He always had time for a kind word to me, you can be sure of that."

As Scrooge said these words, he realized that he rarely made time for his own clerk, Bob Cratchit. The spirit guessed his thoughts but asked anyway.

"What's the matter?"

"Oh, nothing really," said Scrooge. "It's just that I'd like to have a word or two with my clerk, Bob Cratchit. That's all."

"My time grows short," said the spirit. "Quick, let's be off."

This time the spirit took him to another Christmas, where old Marley was lying at death's door.

"Oh, spirit," Scrooge gasped in horror as he looked upon the dying man. "Remove me from this place. Show me no more, I can't bear it."

"I told you I would show you shadows of the things that have happened in your life. They are what they are. Do not blame me."

"Please, spirit," Scrooge pleaded. "Take me back, take me back."

Suddenly, Scrooge lost control. He grabbed the spirit by the shoulders and began shaking it. The spirit did not fight back, for it was only a spirit and could put up no resistance. Scrooge continued shaking it until, without knowing how, he found himself back in his own bed. The spirit was gone. Scrooge lay still for a moment and then sank into a heavy sleep.

The Ghost of Christmas Present

Loud bellows of laughter woke Scrooge in the middle of the night. He looked at the clock on his nightstand and noted the hour—one o'clock!

"Ebenezer Scrooge," a voice called from another room. "Come in, come in and know me better, man."

Scrooge hurried out of bed and shuffled toward the next room. It looked very much like his own bedroom, but it was strangely transformed. Holly, mistletoe, and ivy hung everywhere. There was a long table in the center of the room upon which great heaps of food lay—assorted types of poultry, juicy meats, luscious mince pies, plum puddings, hot chestnuts, rich, ripe fruits, and much more. It was a feast fit for a king. At the head of the table sat a giant of a ghost dressed in fine red robes trimmed in fur, wearing a holly wreath upon his head.

"Come in." The ghost beckoned. "Come in, I say."

Scrooge entered the room cautiously, but the spirit's kind face and his jovial manner gradually lessened the old man's fear.

"I am the Ghost of Christmas Present," announced the spirit. "Please, come closer. Fear me not."

"Spirit," said Scrooge. "Take me where you will. I know you've come here tonight to teach me some sort of lesson."

"As you wish," said the spirit. "Touch my robe."

"Gladly," Scrooge said, as he clasped onto the rich garment.

And with that, the two were lifted beyond the walls and out into the clear, cold, winter air. It was Christmas Day. Lights twinkled everywhere. There were children on sleds, playing in the snow.

"Do you see that house over there?" The spirit pointed.

"Yes I do," Scrooge answered. "It's the humble home of my clerk, Bob Cratchit."

"Come, let's go closer," said the spirit.

"A Merry Christmas to us all, my dears, a Merry Christmas to us all," said Bob as Scrooge and the spirit peeked through the window. Then, a small voice as tiny as its owner was heard. "God bless us, everyone."

"Oh, yes, Tiny Tim. God bless us, every one," said the father, gazing with love at his little son sitting perched upon his shoulder. Young Tim was a cripple, but he never failed to bring joy and gladness into the Cratchit home. Though he needed a crutch to walk and couldn't play in the snow like other children, he never complained. As the family proceeded to sit at the table to share the humble Christmas dinner before them, Scrooge and the spirit continued to look on. Presently, Scrooge asked the ghost a question.

"Tell me, spirit, if Tiny Tim will live."

"I see an empty stool near the chimney corner," the ghost replied, "and a crutch without an owner. If these shadows remain, the child will die."

"Oh no," Scrooge protested. "Say he'll live. Say he'll live."

But the Ghost of Christmas Present had no comfort to give the distraught man. He proceeded to take Scrooge to other homes and places, showing him misery and want as well as happiness.

The Ghost of Christmas Yet to Come

As the bell in the church tower struck twelve, the spirit vanished, and a new and different specter appeared. It came slowly and quietly toward Scrooge. It was dressed in a deep, black garment that shrouded it from head to toe. Scrooge could see nothing of the specter's body or face, except for one outstretched hand that beckoned the old man to follow.

"Yes, I know," said Scrooge, "you're the Ghost of Christmas Yet to Come. I fear you more than any specter I've seen, but I know your purpose is to do me good. Lead on, spirit. I'll follow."

The spirit moved ever so slowly and said not a word. At length, it led Scrooge to a deserted graveyard and then, to a neglected tombstone covered by weeds. One long, bony finger pointed to the stone and Scrooge stepped forward to examine it.

"Whose stone is this, spirit, whose stone?"

The spirit merely nodded and pointed yet again.

Scrooge knelt obediently beside the stone, pushed the weeds aside and rubbed the dirt away to reveal the writing beneath. The old man gasped in horror when he saw his own name engraved on the stone.

"EBENEZER SCROOGE!" he cried. "Oh no, good spirit. It can't be. I'm not the man I was. I'll not be the man I must have been. Good spirit, pity me. Show me that I may change these shadows of the future that you show me. I promise to honor Christmas in my heart, and I'll try to keep the spirit all year. Oh, please, good spirit, tell me that I may wipe off the writing of this terrible stone."

Scrooge went on and on, begging the spirit to show mercy. Then he collapsed on the ground heaving great sobs.

Suddenly, the spirit extinguished itself, and Scrooge found himself in a room that looked strangely familiar.

"This bedpost," he said in amazement, "it's my own. This bed, it's my own, my very own! This room. It's my own room. Oh, Jacob Marley, heaven and Christmas time be praised for this."

Old Scrooge could scarcely contain his joy. He jumped out of bed and began dancing merrily about the room. The tassle on the end of his nightcap swung back and forth. He felt like the young schoolboy he once was, yet even happier than he'd been then.

He rushed his way to the window, and opened it wide, to breathe in the fresh, cold air. There was a young boy in the street below and Scrooge yelled down to him.

"Hello, young lad."

"Hello," the boy answered.

"Can you tell me what day this is?" Scrooge queried.

"Today?" the boy asked, a bewildered expression on his face at being asked such a foolish question. "Why, it's Christmas Day!"

"CHRISTMAS DAY!" Scrooge yelped in delight. "I haven't missed it. The spirits have done it all in one night."

The boy continued staring up at Scrooge, thinking what a silly old fool the man was.

"Do you know the poultry shop in town?" Scrooge asked the boy.

"Indeed I do sir."

"Well," Scrooge continued, "do you know if they've sold the prize turkey that was hanging in the window?"

"It's hanging there now," said the boy.

"Is it?" Scrooge asked. "Well, go on and buy it."

"Are you joking?"

"Oh no, no, no, I'm being earnest. Come back with the poulterer in less than five minutes and I'll give you half a crown."

The boy was delighted. "I'll be back with him quicker than you can say Jack Robinson." And with that, the lad rushed off. Scrooge thought to himself that he would have the turkey delivered to Bob Cratchit's home.

"He won't know who sent it," Scrooge said aloud, "but he'll be delighted. It will make a wonderful Christmas dinner."

Scrooge hurriedly washed and put on his Sunday best. Then off to church he went, wishing everyone he saw a Merry Christmas. Most of the villagers were quite perplexed; they did not know quite what to

make of this new Scrooge. They'd never seen him smiling so, and he'd never before had a kind word for any of them. But off he went, patting children on the head, tipping his hat to the ladies, and stopping to give a few coins to the street beggars.

After church, it was off to his nephew Fred's house for Christmas dinner. "Oh, won't they be delighted to see me," Scrooge thought to himself. And indeed they were.

"Why, Uncle Scrooge!" exclaimed his nephew Fred. "How good of you to come. We're planning a wonderful party, wonderful games, and wonderful happiness." And with that, Fred ushered his uncle in to meet and make merry with the other guests, who were all quite astounded to see that Scrooge had come to join them for Christmas dinner.

The next day Scrooge had planned to be at the office early. If he could only catch Bob Cratchit coming in late—why, that was the thing he'd set his heart on. And he did, yes he did. Cratchit was a full eighteen minutes and a half behind his time. The clerk rushed in the door, scurried to his desk, and set himself to work immediately, hoping that Scrooge would not notice. But the master was waiting for him. Scrooge approached the clerk's desk and said, "What do you mean by coming in at this hour?"

"Oh, I'm so sorry, sir. I know I'm behind my time."

"Yes, indeed you are," Scrooge snarled.

"Well, you see, sir," Bob answered, his voice trembling, "I was making rather merry yesterday, sir. This shall not be repeated, I assure you."

"I tell you what, my young fellow," Scrooge said, "I'm not going to stand for this sort of thing any longer, and therefore . . . therefore . . . *I'm about to raise your salary!*"

"Oh, sir," Bob said in wonderment.

"A Merry Christmas, Bob Cratchit."

"Oh, Merry Christmas, sir."

"A merrier Christmas, Bob, my good fellow, than I've wished you in many a year. I'll not only raise your salary, but I'll endeavor to assist your struggling family. And now, you go and make up that fire before you dot another *i*, Bob Cratchit."

"Yes, sir," Bob said happily. He could hardly believe the change in his master.

Scrooge did it all and more. He became as good a friend, as good a master, and as good a man as the good old city knew. And to Tiny Tim, who did not die, he became like a second father. He spent many days with the boy and grew to love him dearly. And it was often said of Ebenezer Scrooge that he knew how to keep Christmas well, if anybody did.

And so, at Christmas time and all through the year, let us remember the words of Tiny Tim. *"God bless us, every one!"*

The Little Drummer Boy

*by KATHERINE DAVIS, HENRY ONORATI,
and HARRY SIMEONE*

Come, they told me,
    Pa Rum Pum Pum Pum,
Our newborn King to see,
    Pa Rum Pum Pum Pum,
Our finest gifts we bring,
    Pa Rum Pum Pum Pum,
Today before the King,
    Pa Rum Pum Pum Pum,
    Rum Pum Pum Pum,
    Rum Pum Pum Pum,
So to honor Him,
    Pa Rum Pum Pum Pum,
When we come.

Baby Gesu, Pa Rum Pum Pum Pum,
I am a poor boy too,
        Pa Rum Pum Pum Pum,
I have no gift to bring,
        Pa Rum Pum Pum Pum
That's fit to give our King,
        Pa Rum Pum Pum Pum
        Rum Pum Pum Pum,
        Rum Pum Pum Pum,
Shall I play for you,
        Pa Rum Pum Pum Pum,
On my drum.

Mary nodded, Pa Rum Pum Pum Pum,
The ox and lamb kept time,
        Pa Rum Pum Pum Pum,
I played my drum for Him,
        Pa Rum Pum Pum Pum,
I played my best for Him,
        Pa Rum Pum Pum Pum,
        Rum Pum Pum Pum,
        Rum Pum Pum Pum . . .

Then He smiled at me,
        Pa Rum Pum Pum Pum,
Me and my drum . . .

The Christmas Spider

by MARGUERITE DE ANGELI

The gray spider worked very hard every day making long strands of silk that he wove into a web in which he caught troublesome flies. But he noticed that everyone turned away from him because, they said, he was so unpleasant to look at with his long crooked legs and furry body. Of course the gray spider didn't believe that, because he had only the kindliest feelings for everybody. One day when he was crossing the stream he looked into the water. There he saw himself as he really was.

"Oh," he thought, "I *am* very unpleasant to look at. I shall keep out of people's way." He was very sad and hid himself in the darkest corner of the stable. There he again began to work as he always had, weaving long strands of silk into webs and catching flies. The donkey and the ox and the sheep who lived in the stable thanked him for his kindness, because now they were no longer bothered with the buzzing flies. That made the spider very happy.

One night, exactly at midnight, the gray spider was awakened by a brilliant light. He looked about and saw that the light came from the manger where a tiny Child lay on the hay. The stable was filled with glory, and over the Child bent a beautiful mother. Behind her stood a man with a staff in his hand, and the ox and the donkey and all the white sheep were down on their knees.

Suddenly a gust of cold wind swept through the stable and the Baby began to weep from the cold. The mother bent over Him but could not cover Him enough to keep Him warm. The little spider took his silken web and laid it at Mary's feet (for it was Mary) and Mary took up the web and covered the Baby with it. It was soft as thistledown and as warm as wool. The Child stopped His crying and smiled at the little gray spider.

Then Mary said, "Little gray spider, for this great gift to the Babe you may have anything you wish."

"Most of all," said the spider, "I wish to be beautiful."

"That I cannot give you," Mary answered. "You must stay as you are for as long as you live. But this I grant you. Whenever anyone sees a spider at evening, he will count it a good omen, and it shall bring him good fortune."

This made the spider very happy, and to this day, on Christmas Eve, we cover the Christmas tree with "angel's hair" in memory of the little gray spider and his silken web.